The Lost Dog

written and photographed
by
Mia Coulton

To Charlie, Joey, Robby and Izzy

Danny's Big Adventure #8

The Lost Dog

Published by:
MaryRuth Books, Inc.

www.maryruthbooks.com

Text copyright © 2017 Mia Coulton
Photographs copyright © 2017 Mia Coulton

Editor: Michelle DiFrangia
Map illustration: Kaye Hood-Tatara

Library of Congress Control Number: 2016918984
ISBN 978-1-62544-201-7

Printed in the United States of America
10 9 8 7 6 5 4 3

SPC/0719/158195

Contents

Lost

Every afternoon,

Dad would have

a cup of coffee.

Every afternoon,

Danny and Norman

would have a biscuit.

And every afternoon,

Dad would look

out the window

and predict the weather.

"Looks like it's going to storm."

One afternoon

there was a knock

on the front door.

"Now who could that be?"
Dad wondered.

Dad went to the door,

Danny went to the door,

Norman went to the door,

to see who knocked.

Dad opened the door.

No one was there.

But there was a picture

of a white and brown dog.

"Oh my!

A dog is lost!

It looks like the dog

that lives behind us,"

Dad said.

"Why don't you boys go out

and look for the lost dog.

He might be scared.

He might be lonely, too."

Amy
school picture
age 10

Amy

Amy was ten years old.

She did not have a brother.

She did not have a sister.

But she did have a dog.

Her dog's name was Spot.

Spot was white
with brown spots.
That's why Amy
named him Spot.

Spot
dog school picture
age 1

Amy loved her dog Spot.

She loved the way

he licked her cheek.

She loved the way

he snuggled in her arms

when she picked him up.

There was nothing,

absolutely nothing,

Amy didn't love about

her dog, Spot.

Amy loved to put Spot
in her doll buggy
and take long walks.
People would stop her
and say,
"I wish my dog would ride
in a buggy."

Or they would say,
"What a cute little dog.
Where did you get him?"
Amy was the happiest
when she was with Spot.

Spot

Spot loved Amy

as much as Amy loved Spot.

Spot also loved to run.

One day Spot thought
it would be fun
to run away and hide.

He wouldn't run too far
but far enough that Amy
would have to come
and look for him.

He was sure
Amy would find him.
It would be a game
of hide and seek,
he thought.

When Amy got home

from school

she ran into the kitchen

and swung her book bag

on a chair.

She called for Spot.

Spot did not come.

She called again.

Spot still did not come.

She called and called.

Then she knew,

Spot was gone.

Amy began to worry.

"What if he got lost?

He will be hungry and lonely,"

she cried out loud.

Amy would have to find him.

Amy looked out the window
and saw her neighbor,
Mrs. Wiggins, walking
with her little dog.
"Mrs. Wiggins," Amy called,
"have you seen Spot?"

"Sure have," she answered.
"That dog loves, loves, loves
to run."

"Which way did he go?"
Amy asked.

"That way," Mrs. Wiggins said,
pointing to the woods.
"Better find him soon.
Looks like it's going to storm."

Signs

Amy had an idea.

She quickly made signs

with a picture of Spot.

She was going to put

the signs everywhere.

Someone must know

where Spot is.

LOST DOG

"SPOT"
call 888-555-444-3333

Amy ran outside

with a handful of her signs.

She stuck them on trees.

She went

to all her neighbors,

knocked on all their doors,

and left a sign.

Amy didn't know it,
but Spot was hiding
under the pine trees
in a yard close by.

Spot watched Amy
put the signs
on the trees.
He watched her
go up to the doors
and knock.

Spot thought it was fun.
Until it wasn't.

He wanted Amy

to find him soon.

He began to whine.

Searching

Danny and Norman

began searching

for the lost dog, Spot.

They looked in the woods.

Norman sniffed the air.

He sniffed the bushes, too.

The lost dog had gone

in the meadow.

Danny and Norman
followed their noses
down a path
in the meadow.
They went this way,
then that way.

Soon they were back

in their yard.

The lost dog

was somewhere

in their yard.

Found

Danny and Norman

looked all around.

That's when they saw

the pine trees moving

back and forth.

When they went

to have a closer look,

out came Spot.

Danny and Norman

and Spot began to bark.

Amy heard the barking

and took off running

in the direction

of all the noise.

"Spot, Spot, is that you?

Come here, Spot!"

Spot heard Amy calling

and ran to her

as fast as he could.

She picked him up,

gave him a big hug

and said,

"I love you.

Let's go home now.

It looks like it's going

to storm."

Spot was happy

to be in Amy's arms

once again.

Amy called

to Danny and Norman,

"Thank you for helping me

find Spot.

Tomorrow I'm going

to bring you

a special treat."

And that is what she did.

THE POND
THE NEW
PARK
THE WOODS
THIS WAY PATH
THAT
DANNY NORMAN'S HOUSE
THE
TREES
THE BIG ROAD